Credits
Visual Advisor: B.J. Bechtel

Help Me Find

My

By Nena Kring

The
journey
is
LONG,
but
the
rewards
are
SWEET.

I invited all of
The letters From
A through to Z,
But looking
Around,
Where could
They be?

You may wonder,
Where are
They going?
And where have
They been?

They're in every
Word in this
book
And even in
G R I N.

2

Please read through the pages.
Put ads in the gazette.
Find all of the letters
In this sly alphabet!
I've checked so many places,
They're really quite quick.
Please give them a tap
With your fingertip.

But don't get distracted,
There's a party to attend.
Catch all of the letters
My quick-fingered friend!

A was in **A**lligator
Where he truly belongs.

Please try to find him, and give him a bonk!

B B was in Bumblebee,
Because it starts with a B.

But off B went running,
Hopping and jumping
And swinging in trees.

C was in Carrot.
That's his usual habit.

But what's all
that racket?
© is talking
with my parrot!

D was in **D**og.

But with a quick
Flip and a roll,
D has gone running
Down the hall!

E was in Elephant,

But now he's not.

E went to find
A shady spot.

F was in Flamingo,

But there he goes.
Now F's knocking on glasses,
Vases and windows.

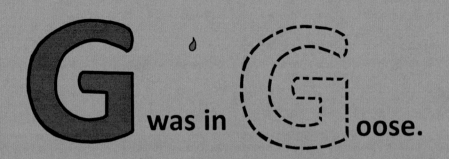

G was in **G**oose.

But since **G** broke loose,

He's snoozing away
In those bamboo shoots.

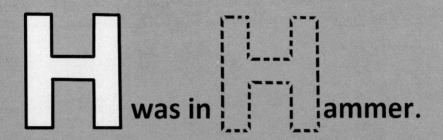

H was in Hammer.

But with a bang and a clamor,

H is now shaking
The party banner!

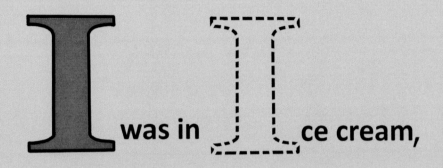

I was in Ice cream,

But he runs free.

Now I is floating
Down the
Crystal clear stream.

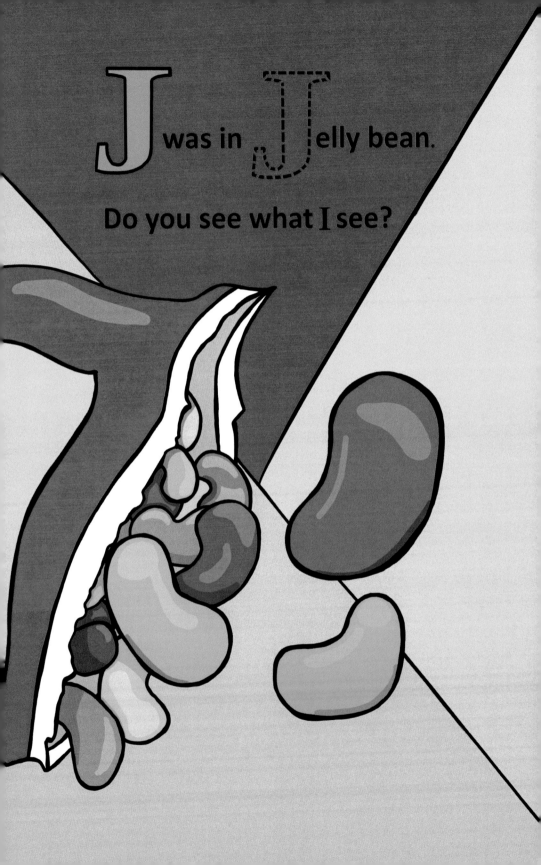

J is now riding
In a bright submarine!

Now K hides behind fences
Thinking he's hidden.

L was in Lizard,

But he's not
A good climber.

Instead,
L admires
Himself in
The mirror.

28

But have no doubts.
M is now on
The old lighthouse.

But now he's
Munching bananas
In the damp
Jungle air.

That O sails a boat
Atop the sea waves.

P P
was in Pirate

But had nowhere to sit.
So, ℙ left that place
For a sunny, warm island.

Q was in Quail

But fell in the pail.

Now you can see Q
Spilling all of the milk!

38

R was in Rabbit,
But I Just couldn't
Grab it.

Now R is hiding
In the jackets!

Dancing around
The hamburger buns!

42

Which letter is next,
I can't quite recall.
Say the ABCs with me
To help find them all.

A B C D

E F G

H I J K

L M N

O P Q R

S T U V

W X Y and Z

What's after S?

Now you see
That we need T!

But T really loves
To dig through the mail.

U is bathing
In the Nutella!

Now V is in the kitchen
Making mashed potatoes.

W was in Whale

But found it quite stale.
He wanted more friends
And so found a snail.

X was in boX, then foX, and T-ReX.

But I could bet
The car seat is next!

Y Y

Y was in Yolk,
But he's funny,
You know.

Y went to the beach
With his friends
And is cracking
Some jokes.

Z was in Zebra,
But he got a bit hungry.

So Z left to get pizza
With pepperoni.

Well, look at that.
You caught them right quick
And sent them all back!

I invited them all,
Letters A through to Z.
So let's call them out now
For the alphabet party!

69

68

NOW, LET'S EAT!

72

Other books in the Adventure Series

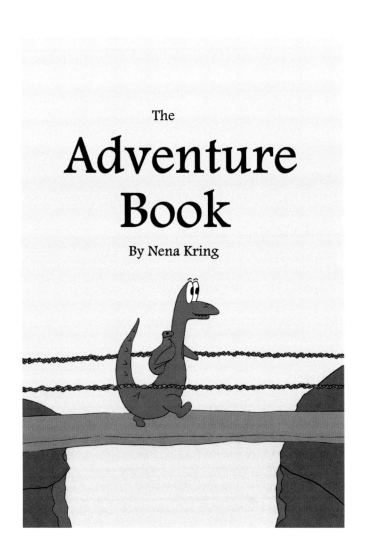

The

Adventure Book

By Nena Kring

Other series by
Nena Kring